SEX FOR SM

SEX FOR SMART WOMEN

ADRIENNE WEST

THOUGHT CATALOG BOOKS

 Published by Thought Catalog Books, a division of The Thought & Expression Co., Williamsburg, Brooklyn.

For general information and submissions: hello@thoughtcatalog.com.

First edition, 2015.

ISBN 978-1515216698

10 9 8 7 6 5 4 3 2 1

Founded in 2010, Thought Catalog is a website and imprint dedicated to your ideas and stories. We publish fiction and non-fiction from emerging and established writers across all genres.

Cover photography by ©iStockPhoto.com/blanaru

Contents

An Introduction and a Dedication

I'm a real girl. Let's get that out of the way. I write about things that happen to me — and they happen to me exactly because I am real. I am not a mousey romance novel character. I'm no Anastasia Steele, shy and demure. I'm a too-much girl — too many curves, too much passion and not enough insecurity to make me "relatable."

When you're a woman you're always taught not to be the too-much girl, it's not ladylike to want something badly — to ask for it or demand it or to feel too strongly about anything. "Whatever you think" is supposed to be our anthem, with a healthy side of "I'm sorry but I think..." on the off chance we want to disagree with someone about something. The Anastasia Steele's of the world are the good girls. They are always feminine and put-together and the protagonist of the story — the one you root for instead of her less virginal friend.

I've had enough of those characters and I think everyone else has too. I think women are smart enough to know you can be flawed and insecure without that being the defining characteristic of your life. I don't want to cheer for these sad, apologetic girls.

So, like I said, these stories are real. They're a collection of the kind of experiences any adventurous girl has or could have if she was so inclined, documented for the sake of having a non-sad, non-woe-is-me female protagonist and dedicated to the kind of woman who has waited for one.

1

Sex Slave

I thought I was looking for a boyfriend when I set up my online dating profile.

I'd never had much luck with dating. It wasn't that I wasn't interested — I'd always loved men. Dating them was fun — the balance between a man's personality and my own feminine one was electric, it kept things interesting. But for whatever reason the relationships never lasted very long. I'd do things like leave town for days without telling him or bringing my phone, or stay in bed with a book all day and forget to answer his texts.

It just wasn't second nature for me to be tied down and predictable.

When I met Paul online I expected the same cycle to occur. We met up at the corner dive bar where I prefer to meet all my first dates. He complimented my lip color — it's always a great sign when a man isn't intimidated by lipstick. He asked me about my writing and told me about messing around with a popular edgy publication when he went to college with the founder. But now he had to keep his distance because he's a lawyer and the legal world is super conservative.

I told him that was too bad, the idea of a guy being associated with something somewhat dangerous was exciting. He smiled mischievously and said, "You have no idea."

Girls don't need tricks to get guys to come home with them at the end of dates but I happen to have an excellent one anyway: I live in a condo along the river in my city. A walk along the river is the perfect nightcap to any date and the guy will always walk me up afterwards, "to make sure I get home safe."

So Paul was sitting on my bed while I made some drinks and thought about whether I wanted to have sex with him that night. I was attracted to him, sure, he was broad shouldered and tall with dark hair and dark eyes I couldn't stop staring into. There was no strong reason not to, I figured, but we may as well wait another date in case he was one of those guys that's weird about first date sex.

That changed fairly quickly.

I handed him his drink and he announced, "I'm going to enjoy this drink while you suck my cock."

"Excuse me?!" I couldn't have possibly heard him correctly.

"This looks like a great drink, and it's going to be even better while you're blowing me." He stopped to take in my negative expression and lifted my head with a single finger under my chin. "A girl like you can make a man really happy. You want to do that, it's what makes you special."

I couldn't deny that he had some sort of power over me at this point. The way he was controlling the situation turned me on and his hand caressing my face stirred up a familiar feeling in my abdomen.

Well, what did I have to lose?

So I obliged him. I set my drink down and kneeled before him, unzipping his pants.

I wasn't surprised to find his cock was larger than average, it's this way with most confident men, like a chicken and egg thing. I flicked my tongue over the head of his penis a few times before I began to take him in my mouth. He watched me coolly, taking a swig of his drink.

Inside somewhere, a deep need to impress him rose. I went to town. I kissed and licked and deep throated. I massaged the sweet spot at the tippy top of his shaft on the underside. I took his balls in my mouth and swirled my tongue around. I gave him my A-game and looked up, searching for approval written on his face. It was there, but not as fully as I'd hoped for.

"To completion," he reminded me.

I slid my hands down his forearms and then grasped his hands, depositing them on the back of my head. This wasn't one of my "moves," I didn't know what I was doing anymore. I was on autopilot now.

He had two fistfuls of my hair, one on each side of my head. He was gentle, but firm as he held me in place, thrusting his hips and pouring himself into my mouth. It was uncomfortable at first, I worried about gagging. But I heard him gasp as he slipped into my throat and I knew this was special for him — he was enjoying himself, losing control, losing himself to me.

I may have been the one kneeling on the floor, but he was at my mercy, he was in ecstasy, and he needed me to feel this way.

I held up my hands, showing him I wasn't going to resist and he groaned loudly in excitement. He thrust faster into my mouth, careful to make his movement fluid. This time I felt his grip tighten on my hair as he didn't allow his dick to slide back out of my mouth. He held me there. I could feel him tensing up so I made an extra effort to hold this position — and I was rewarded with his loudest groan yet and a mouthful of salty cum.

I swallowed and licked my lips. I felt satisfied somehow.

He grinned and stared down at me. "I told you you would like it."

He laid down on my bed and I instantly curled up next to him. I felt happy and comfortable. With my head on his chest I reached up and began massaging his scalp, my weird need to please this man had not been satiated.

"What do you want?" I asked him.

"I want to come over two or three times a week and stand over you and fuck your throat. I don't want to jerk off anymore."

I gulped. This was definitely not what I was looking for. It was sleazy. "What if I want more than that?"

"But you don't want more. You just think you're supposed to want more. Did you hear yourself earlier? You told me you don't like being tied down. And look at you, look at how your body responded to being my sex slave."

He quickly reached down and knocked my thighs apart. Before I could register what he was doing his fingers were inside me and my back was arched. Holy shit, I gasped as he masterfully, rhythmically rubbed my gspot with the tip of his finger.

I looked down at him to see that he was hard again and grinned.

He got up and kneeled between my legs and pulled me up, so my butt was resting on his thighs, legs wrapped around his waist.

"I am going to fuck you and then we'll sleep here together and you'll see. This is better than dating — to give ourselves to each other completely."

I nodded. This was exciting, and what else was I going to do tonight?

He grabbed his drink off the nightstand and poured a bit into my mouth before kissing me and sucking the taste of whiskey off my tongue. He trailed the dewy glass down my neck to my collarbone and I shivered. He took the remaining ice cube and deposited it in his mouth before leaning down and kissing my nipple. It was the most divine sensation, heat and ice.

I felt his hips move under mine and his cock sliding around my wet pussy, but not entering. I always loved it when guys did this, the anticipation was unbearable, in an addictive way. It made time stand still.

"You're such a good girl, Adrienne," he mumbled as he kissed my neck, clearly enjoying himself. I lifted my hips to meet his and he drove his cock deep inside me. That moment — the first time it goes in — is always the best. It reminds me why we do such crazy stuff for sex, it really is that good.

I'd consider his offer later. He didn't need an answer now. He just needed me to be here, writhing with pleasure as he had his way with me.

2

My Best Friend's Dad

He was the first guy to ever get his cock to that place in the back of my mouth where it can slip into my throat. It was an exhilarating discovery, learning there's a whole new thing out there to try and do. I was surprised no one had tried this with me before, from what I can gather after the fact it seems very popular with men, but I guess most are too intimidated to try it in real life, or at least initiate it.

My best friend in college had a lake house about an hour away from our campus. We'd go there a few times a semester with our group of girlfriends and whatever guys we were dating or crushing on at the moment and spend the weekend playing drinking games and daring each other to go skinny dipping. It was a college student's dream.

I met her dad the same day I met her, as he lugged her heavy furniture into our freshman dorm, I thought he was sweaty and attractive — in a rugged, masculine way. His name was Steve and he bought us burgers later that day, after we'd all finished moving.

"Has anyone ever told you your dad is really hot?"

I asked this when we were going to bed that night, figuring a little salacious question asking would bond us (it did). "Ha ha, are you one of those girls? I don't get the whole "hot dad" thing. They're just old. I like them young. I dated a junior last year."

It was the last conversation we had about him, but it definitely wasn't the last time I thought about him. I always made sure to dress my best when I knew he was stopping by. Little dresses only a college freshman could wear, low cut tank tops and once — when I was especially bored — a sheer white t-shirt with no bra underneath because, “whoops” I had just rolled out of bed.

It was a fun game to play but I didn’t think he ever noticed, or at least he never really acknowledged me until one of those debaucherous weekends when my friend and her dad got their messages crossed and we all ended up at the lake house together. At first it was uncomfortable when we arrived and saw the trucks, Steve was there with his brother and some other men. They had planned a fishing weekend. But, Steve gave us a wink and told us to stay on the lower level and he’d stay out of our way. Everyone felt relieved and told my BFF how lucky she was to have a “cool” dad. But I felt something else when Steve winked at us.

That night, after many, many drinks I found myself wandering out to the dock. Everyone else had passed out, but I was wide awake. I saw Steve approaching me from the winding path down the hill from the cabin, two bottled beers in one hand. He handed one to me wordlessly, searching my eyes for something — the reason I was awake and alone, maybe.

We stood there silently until he stepped forward and brushed my hair off my face, “You’re a beautiful girl, Adrienne, don't think that goes unnoticed." I blushed, could he tell I was harboring a crush on him? Did he notice the way I jerked slightly at his touch, nervous about my body's powerful response to it?

"Thanks Steve," I said, taking a swig of my beer and looking at the moonlight reflecting over the waves. When I dared to make eye contact with him again I realized he hadn't moved, he was still watching me intently. Did this mean — before I could finish my thought, he was on me, one hand placed very firmly on my lower back the other in my hair as he kissed me. Before I knew what was happening, his tongue was in my mouth tracing mine.

I got the urge to wrap my legs around him, but there was nowhere to balance on this dock. He must have noticed this fact.

"Come up to my bedroom." It was a request, but it was also a statement, he was sure of my answer.

I giggled when we crossed the threshold and closed the door behind us. It wasn't just that when he grinned and you could see the wrinkles around his eyes, it wasn't just the physical attraction. It was his demeanor, it was that he was a real live man, not a flimsy college boy. This was going to be a different kind of hook-up.

"You're married," I reminded him, not particularly pleased about remembering this detail myself.

"I can keep a secret," he said, closing his mouth on mine again, and backing us to the bed.

He removed all my clothing fairly quickly and then he laid on top of me, fully clothed. The rough textures rubbing against my bare skin felt incredible. "I can't believe this is happening," he laughed. "I've wanted this for a very long time."

I wanted to prove that I was worth it, all this risk. So I reached up and felt him through his pants, staring longingly into his eyes. He pulled his shirt over his head as I unbuckled, unzipped, and released a very healthy looking cock.

I slid off the bed and onto the floor to get a better angle and he stood over me gathering my hair behind my head as I started blowing him. I looked up at him and was rewarded with a face that was most definitely in ecstasy as I took him in my mouth.

He held my head down on his cock while I took him in deeply. This was a move widely hated by every woman I knew, but it was usually performed by dumb frat guys. Steve knew what he was doing, he was looking out for me and making the experience short — just long enough to add a bit of excitement. When he pulled out of me he smiled and leaned down to kiss me. "I knew you'd be very good at this."

He pulled me up and walked me over to a dresser placed underneath a large window. I could still see the moonlight on the lake as he bent me over it. Was it really just a few moments ago we were nearly strangers on that dock together? I was brought back to reality by Steve spreading my legs further apart and pushing my upper back down until my bare breasts were pressed against its cool surface and I felt him enter me.

"Oh my god..." I couldn't help but moan as he thrust into me. He shushed me by placing his hand over my mouth for a moment as he picked up speed. My moan was apparently too loud but he was willing to risk the loud sound it made as he slapped my ass over and over, groaning and filling me with his cock.

I couldn't believe how turned on this was making me. I was no virgin but I'd never experienced sex like this — it wasn't awkward or embarrassing or rushed. I was very aware that I was getting fucked by a Man, not "fooling around" with a boy.

"Are you on birth control?" He asked and when I answered yes, he cooed, "good girl." The sound of that phrase coming out of his mouth sent me over the edge and I felt myself spasming around his cock as I released myself into my orgasm, even enjoying the sensation of a bit of extra liquid rolling down my thigh.

He was still thrusting into me rhythmically, alternating between kneading my breasts and grabbing — and slapping — my ass. I hadn't had sex last this long before and I loved being able to savor the feeling. "I'm getting close," he groaned and I tensed my body up, holding my place more firmly so that he could get deeper inside me as he unloaded his semen into me.

"You're very good at this, but I can tell you're just a beginner," he began as we laid in his bed to rest. I laughed, it was true. I had this fantasy about being a girl who gave amazing head and being really good at all the sex stuff, like some kind of femme fatale men couldn't resist. "I can sense you want to learn though." I nodded in agreement, wondering if he could read my mind. I could play out this crush and learn what would drive my next actual boyfriend wild — who wouldn't want to kill those two birds with one stone?

And so, I began a year-long affair with Steve. We'd sneak away for a weekend when I said I was visiting my parents and meet at the lake house for lessons — how to stimulate differently for a long or slow blow job, which positions let him get in the deepest while still providing some kind of external stimulation for me, how to prepare for and receive anal, how to lie with my head falling off the edge of the bed and allow him to push his cock into my throat (without choking). Occasionally I just gave him head while he drove me around campus, careful not to drive anywhere too well-lit or populated.

I never told my best friend about the affair, we'd ended it when the luster wore off at the end of the school year. By that point I think we both got what we wanted from the relationship, and had a lifetime's worth of steamy sex. But every time I visit a cabin or a lake house I can't help but think of that first night, where he showed me so many possibilities.

3

Blow Job Lessons from My Best Friend's Dad

Of all the memories I have of being 19 and having an affair with my best friend's dad, the one that I think about most often is the first blow job lesson he gave me. He loved oral, both giving and receiving, and he wanted to make sure I knew how to enjoy both.

"For most guys truly good head is a once in a lifetime thing. If you know how to do it right, a guy will remember you for the rest of his life."

He said this to me before we really started

anything serious, we were in his bed after sex just talking, and he was going on about the value of good oral.

The idea intrigued me greatly, most of my friends hated giving head — or at least hated doing it for more than a few minutes. I was interested in approaching the whole thing a bit differently. I didn't want to hate doing something the guy I was with loved. It seemed like a source of endless friction. I wanted a kind of explosive partnership that was much more intentional about mutually being the best for your partner than passively hoping for their infallibility.

I don't like the middle of the road, if I was going to do something at all, I wanted to do all of it — be the best at it, or at least take it to it's farthest end and experience it fully. Why be a bear at all if you're not going to be a grizzly? When I was younger I denied myself cream and sugar for a long time, until I learned to love the taste of coffee without it, and now I'll never need cream or sugar. When something is good for you, you just have to learn how to love it.

All this to say, he wanted to give me blow job lessons, and I was ready to be a very good student.

I knew that not every man was going to like what Steve liked, but I figured it would be easiest to adjust from guy to guy when I at least knew one really well. Like how learning your second foreign language is a lot easier than learning your first.

One afternoon I was packing an overnight bag to meet Steve at his lake house when he texted me:

> You'll learn about blow jobs tonight. Come very hydrated.

I grabbed a water bottle and sipped-drank it on the short drive to the lake house. When I parked I saw he was waiting for me. Seated on the porch with his back against one of the cedar posts, reading something, or pretending to read at least while he waited for me. He looked so handsome like that.

"How's school?" he asked. I laughed, it was so funny to him that I was a student, that I was so much younger than him. It turned me on as well — and I couldn't tell if it was his pleasure at the situation or my own curiosity about someone with a few decades of experience on me.

He poured us some wine inside the house and I drank nervously — he always made me nervous, it was part of his charm. Even when we just talked he stood closer to me than a person normally would. It intimidated and excited me. I took a step back and hopped up on the counter, he stood between my legs and kissed me, wrapping his arms around me and pulling me into him tightly, making the kiss more urgent than casual. I wanted to lay on the counter and feel his weight on top of me right then, but I knew that wasn't his plan for the night.

"Can we just have sex first?" I asked, a bit breathless from his advance and finding an irresistible urge inside me to get a quick fix in.

"No..." He moved from kissing my mouth to my neck. "It's good to delay gratification a bit. It makes it better, you'll see." It was impossible to see how he could be right, but all I could do was try to persuade him through other means. Maybe if I started to rub his cock he'd be overcome by the same lust that was making my brain fuzzy. I reached my hand down and felt him, he was definitely hard. But he merely grabbed my hand and deposited it back on the counter.

He made us cook dinner then. I've never seen anyone look so sexy while dicing vegetables but I couldn't think about anything else. Everything was sex. Chopping vegetables was sex. Stirring a sauce was sex. Watching his mouth while he drank wine was sex.

I was quiet while we ate. I preferred to stare at his mouth and hands and fantasize about the place on my body I'd put them rather than make polite conversation. As if he could read my mind he was patient with my silence, the corners of his mouth turning up when he caught me lost in thought, my eyes focused on him.

I placed my dishes by the sink after dinner, expecting him to tell me we had to clean up first, too. But I felt his mouth on the back of my neck, his arm reaching around me stomach and pulling me backwards into his body. He reached one hand forward and cupped me between my legs and I felt myself coming undone with anticipation.

"Let's go upstairs."

He brought me to his bed where he sat, and I kneeled in front of him. He looked so loving when he looked at me.

"You should always start playfully. Don't be too quick at it. You should act like all you want in the world is for the guy to cum, but you're not in a big hurry to get it over with. Run your tongue around the edge of the head, especially on the underside.

And then when you start taking it in your mouth, hide your teeth behind your lips."

I did all these things for a moment, it felt a bit disjointed but I noticed his hips writhing a bit and it became more natural, more fun. It wasn't my first blow job, but it was my first time trying to do something specific, or even trying really hard at it.

I tried to remember what he said and smiled internally (something someone told me about coming off as having a good time once) before running my lips up and down his shaft, pausing at the tip to lick my way around it and then taking more of it in my mouth, swirling my tongue around it when I slowly pulled it out.

He stood up then, and steadied my head between his hands while he helped me get the rhythm down, pushing himself in and out of my mouth.

He stopped me while I was catching my breath and lifted my face with a few fingers under my chin. "Men want to admire your face while you're doing this. You look so good with my cock in your mouth," he pushed himself back in my mouth, watching me intently as he pushed himself in and out again. He must have been right, I'd never seen his face look like this before. He was so focused, even if just to memorize the moment.

"Curl your tongue, make a snug bed for my cock." "Cup the balls. Don't play with them separately, but as a unit." I followed his instructions.

All of this is, I guess, considered a warm-up. When he's really ready to start Steve told me coordination is important. I needed to move my mouth in sync with my hands so it felt like one thing was happening instead of two separate things.

"See if you can catch your breath while you still keep it in your mouth. Just relax your lips over just the head and pull on it, breathe through your nose."

I tried this and it was unexpectedly easy — but probably because I knew he was expecting me to stop and test this out.

"You can always ask a man what he likes you to do. I like to get deep inside. I want to feel your throat. It mimics sex, but it's more relaxing. And more exciting." I was nervous about this part, but the good kind of nervous, because I knew I'd be happy I did it. And he made me feel very safe. I took him back in my mouth and allowed him to move his hips forward while holding me in place. This is where I discovered my own trick, when I resisted my urge to back off, I found my mouth suddenly filled with my own saliva. My body produced more of what I needed when I pushed it to the edge, and I suddenly had lube for my hand to run up and down his shaft.

He wrapped his hand around mine and showed me the speed and firmness he liked, keeping his other hand on the back of my head to keep us in sync, every few moments removing our hands and hitting my throat with his cock.

"When I speed up, it means you're doing a good job. I'm getting closer," he told me, as he sped up our routine.

He told me that some guys like you to go until completion and others just want to warm up for sex, they want the act of finishing inside you, it's a primal instinct. He was of the latter persuasion.

"When a man says he's about to cum, keep doing what you are doing, and if he is guiding you, let him take over. He knows what he needs."

I removed my hand from his cock and ran them up and down his thighs to signal that I was willing to do this. I looked up at him as I suddenly felt salty precum in my mouth. He was looking at me intently, pumping in and out of his mouth. I struggled not to move even though his groans were really turning me on. Finally I felt him break rhythm and push himself deep inside my mouth, depositing his semen down the back of it. It was always a bit difficult not to gag with the surprise of a guy cumming in your mouth, but since it was so far back, it was easier as it was already being swallowed by the time I realized what was happening.

He fell back onto the bed behind him. "Godddddd Adrienne, you're already very good at this."

This wasn't the last blow job lesson, we usually practiced before sex from then on, but they got quicker — which I took as a compliment.

4

Sex Toys for Smart People

When I was having an affair with my best friend's dad, he liked to have his dick inside me even when we weren't actively having sex. Isn't that weird? He said he liked the idea of me being "full."

He'd have me sit on his lap at the desk in his lake house facing away from him, towards the large monitor on his desk. He'd make me try to write papers that way, for as long as I could stand it. I wasn't supposed to move my hips at all or ride him, but the impulse once he was inside me was almost uncontrollable. I couldn't stand not to.

"Just a few lines," he'd say.

"I literally can't make my brain function right now."

It was the truth. How could I make any sense of Schopenhauer with my cloudy sex brain. It was like trying to write high — I didn't have the clarity or the desire to do anything but give in to temptation.

I'd wiggle a little bit and pretend it was an accident, or that I was just adjusting. The sensation made it difficult for him too. I'd take his hands in mine and trail them along my thighs, or use them to cup my breasts, my hands on his. This was cheating too, but he was more lenient about it. And it worked him up to the point where he'd start moving his hips too and we could finally start having sex the way my whole body was screaming for us too.

When he was more stern he'd lift me off of his lap and slap my ass before making me start all over. I loved it.

He fantasized about holding me like this while I gave oral to another guy. Something about feeling like I was his and he could do whatever he wanted to with me, even have me pleasure someone else. I couldn't deny that the idea did something pleasing to me when I visualized it, but I was young then and we had enough new stuff to try. Now I wished I'd let him.

Another time he guided my rhythm the entire time by pinching my nipples as I rode him this way. Pinching and pulling them away from my body to signal me to move forward, or relaxing his fingers so I could move back.

One day I showed up and he had a present for me. A rectangular box with a little bow wrapped around it.

I smiled. This was sweet.

"What is it?"

"I bought you a gift. Something for us to do tonight." A sex toy?

When I unwrapped it I was confused. It was a puzzle. Not even a very difficult one, just a 50-piece one of a photo of Degas' Trefl Dancers in Blue, my favorite.

I searched his face, trying to figure out what was going on. Was he injured? Were we not hooking up this weekend?

"You're going to do this puzzle while you sit in my lap like a good girl."

I groaned. I don't think he understood how difficult this was going to be for me.

"I bought you an easy one, you're smart, it won't take you long. And then you'll get a reward." He could be so cheesy.

"I'll try. But I won't be able to finish it."

We stripped and he sat down at a chair in front of the dining room table, the puzzle spread out in front of him. He pulled me toward him by my hips and slid a hand between my legs, slowly tracing the outline of my clit, warming me up. "I love watching you try not to enjoy yourself," it was a mumble, he was focused on my lady parts. Pulling me closer he kissed the top area outside my labia with a soft peck and then slid his tongue in between my lips. I couldn't receive oral standing up, my knees always buckled so he left it at that, turning me around so I could slowly lower myself onto him.

This was always the worst part. Any girl will tell you one of the best parts of sex is the very first time a guy's cock goes into you. That initial insertion — when you remember exactly how fucking great sex feels.

I immediately wanted to bounce or grind or otherwise do anything to cause friction, but I knew

I was in this for the long haul tonight. So I sat there, perched on his lap, trying to ignore every biological impulse that millions of years of evolution has put in my body, working on a damn puzzle.

I managed to put at least three pieces together with each corner piece before I turned around to gauge Steve's facial expression. The slight movement triggered me, I realized I felt very slippery, this whole anticipation thing was working. He stared back at me, focused. He wasn't breaking.

I hated this. I could smell him when I was this close — he always smelled intoxicating, not like a spray or anything just manly — like soap and sweat. I was so close to scratching my itch, he was already there, just thrust a few times, use one of those big masculine hands to help a girl out. Come on.

I tried to do the puzzle faster. Lining up the edge pieces that went along with the corners so I had a skeleton. It's a small puzzle, not much left. I focused on the dancer's faces, there were only so many pieces with the face and hair on them and it was easy to see how they went together specifically.

He moved his hands from my hips to my ass and just moved them around, rubbing and grabbing as the fancy struck him. I squirmed.

"Up."

I stood up slowly, feeling how slick his dick was as it came out of me.

"Lean forward."

I obliged, grabbing the sides of the table. He spanked me.

"Sit back down now. Try not to move, Adrienne."

The hard part again. I grabbed his cock and guided it into me again as I sat. I needed to finish this.

Despite knowing what his answer would be, I urged him anyway, "Can we please finish after? I want to fuck you so bad."

"You're almost done, and besides, I'm enjoying the view." His hands were rubbing my ass again. I couldn't help but move a little. He didn't stop me this time. He was losing control too. He always got off on spanking me. I could goad him into finishing me off.

"You know how fucking sexy I think you are

when you're slapping my ass. You can feel how wet you make me."

His breathing became slower, more deliberate. I started to move slightly, and again, he didn't stop me. He silently let me continue my dirty talk persuasion.

"You have no idea how fucking bad I want you to fuck me right now. I need you." I never felt confident that my dirty talk was actually sexy but I just said whatever came into my head and he seemed to like it, so I kept going.

"Come on, fuck me." With that last urge, he finally broke.

I took his hands and mine and placed one on my breast, making him grab me and the other between my legs, forcing his middle finger to rub my clit. He started moving underneath me, inching forward and back.

"Fuck."

He lifted me up and I swept all those puzzle pieces off the table and climbed on, laying on my back. He grabbed my legs and pulled me forward so that my butt was on the very edge of the table. Holding my legs far apart he again entered me, this time with purpose, pumping hard.

I reached down and rubbed myself as he thrusted into me. The pleasure was already spreading through my body — maybe there was something to this delayed gratification thing. He groaned, he enjoyed watching me touch myself and being able to pleasure himself with my body while he did.

I could feel him pulsing inside me as he picked up speed, the anticipation of his imminent orgasm put me over the edge. I stretched one hand on the table behind my head as I moaned and arched my back as far as I could on the hard table, finally giving into my body. Steve dropped my legs and bent down, resting his elbows on either side of me so he could feel my body underneath his as he came. With a final thrust I felt him cum, making an extremely pleasurable sound as he did, his mouth pressed just below my ear, breathing heat onto my neck.

Afterwards we put the puzzle pieces back in the box and I forgot about it until I got a package with no return address on it a few weeks later. It was the completed puzzle, framed. Something to hang on my dorm room wall and feel a twinge of excitement from every time I look at it.

5

My Personal Trainer

From the beginning I should say that I don't usually go for muscle-y guys, or even "hot" guys. I crave a particular kind of dirty hot that escapes most sought-after modern men. They're too pretty.

But every now and then I catch a glimpse of a perfectly chiseled torso and I get it. It feels very animalistic to admire great abs and anything that makes you feel primal also makes you feel sexy. This shirtless image makes me feel like, yes, this is the human form in its most perfect condition and I would not at all mind being underneath it.

This is all to say when I met my physical trainer I was not intimidated by his striking appearance or his Zac Efron abs. Of course he was going to be hot, it was his full-time job to look ridiculous. Like being an underwear model but with more busy work. I greeted him with, "I think you should know that I hate working out." I thought he'd laugh or at least smile, but he just locked eyes with me and said, very seriously, "That's not good."

My heart sank. I had signed up for a personal trainer because I did hate working out. I didn't even know how to use a gym. I'd played soccer in school and I loved playing a game, but I had always hated the workouts involved. Now that I was out of school and writing full-time, I spent way too much time sitting on my ass to not learn how. I foolishly hoped he would take it easy on me.

"You're going to start by emailing me every night to tell me everything you ate that day."

"Oh," I replied, "I don't think I have an issue with my diet, I'm just looking to learn how to stay in shape."

"No. I need to review what you are putting into your body. It affects what I will have you do in our sessions." He was so serious.

And so I began ending every night with an email to my stoic trainer, John. I tried to be conversational, explaining anything that looked too unhealthy:

Hi John,

Here's my food for the day:

Breakfast:

1 egg white/1 egg

slice of cheddar cheese

sriracha

Lunch:

1 slice wheat bread

turkey/lettuce/mayo

1 bag pop chips

1 chocolate donut (a coworker brought them in for her birthday)

Snack:

string cheese

Dinner:

Cheeseburger and 1/4 serving of fries (it was a first date, I couldn't order a salad!)

No response. He never responded. He only

looked at me disapprovingly when it came time for our weekly session. "Adrienne, you're going to stick to your meal plan this week. Or else I'm going to be forced to punish you next session."

"Isn't working out punishment enough?"

"You haven't seen anything yet." He smirked. It was the first time I'd seen anything resembling a smile. He looked good.

It was then that I realized how attracted to him was.

I'd thought about him all week, how I needed to impress him by sticking to my meal plan or by including a funny comment at the end of my email — and how he didn't crack until he talked about punishing me. What did he even mean?

That second training session was harder than the first. Instead of just showing me a bunch of machines and how to use them, we did a circuit, and he watched me complete each rep. I was laying on a bench lifting small dumbbells over my head when I noticed how low he wore his pants. His hands were outstretched spotting me, causing his t-shirt to lift up a bit and exposing a few inches of his very lower abdomen. I think my jaw dropped a bit as I did a double take over his exposed body and up to his smirking face.

Shit. He caught me staring.

He was almost laughing now as he told me to get up. It was time for the treadmill. I followed him, groaning internally. "I'm going to push the buttons for you, you're not to touch them. Got it?"

What did he mean?

"What if I need to run slower?" I asked him.

"Adrienne, I know what I'm doing. You're going to need to trust me."

He started me off at 4.0. I could almost walk.

"This is a good pace," I laughed.

"Nah, you're just warming up."

He's an expert, I thought, just trust him this one time and see what happens. And so I did, and it was really an incredible workout. I ran faster and harder than I ever would have on my own and it sucked — but I stuck with it.

"I think I can see a little bit about why people do this for fun," I told him.

"I told you you'd like it," He said grinning playfully. "Now go hit the showers and I'll see you here next week." With that he slapped my ass, turned, and walked back towards the trainer's desk. What?

What was he thinking? You can't just slap a woman's ass? That's like, sexual harassment or something. Plus, I was paying him money. The whole thing was weird. I should have been upset, but I wasn't. In fact, if I was honest with myself, I was giddy.

I showered at the gym and replayed the moment a hundred times. Had he tried to pat me on the back and grossly misjudged the distance? Was it a force of habit from his football days? By the time I'd dried myself off and dressed again I'd convinced myself that it was a mistake. A meaningless mistake.

But I caught his eye as I walked from the locker room to the front entrance. And I could have sworn he winked.

The next week I was vigilant with my meal plan. I wanted to impress John. I wanted him to be proud of me.

Hi John,

This is what I ate today:

Breakfast:

2 egg whites, 1 egg

onion and red pepper
1/3 cup skim milk

Lunch:
1 whole wheat wrap
1 chicken breast
1 cup mixed peppers
fajita seasoning

Snack:
1/4 cup almonds

Dinner:
1 chicken breast
2 cups broccoli
4 tbsp soy sauce
1 cup strawberries

Hope your week is going well 🙂

I used a god damn smiley face and he still didn't respond. But I knew he'd have an opinion on my improvement, I just needed to wait until our session.

To my surprise, when I emailed him my final food log before our meeting, he responded:

Adrienne,

The gym is undergoing routine maintenance this afternoon. I moved our session to 10pm.

John

Of course this seemed suspicious. Of course it did. At least, I wanted it to be suspicious. I wanted it to be a farce, for this to be some made up reason for him to get me alone while the gym was deserted. But I couldn't be sure. John was so stoic. And he was perfect looking. Why would he be interested in me?

But I spent extra time getting ready that night anyway. I wore new capri workout leggings that hugged my curves and I showered beforehand, so that my hair was clean and bouncy in my long pony. As I drove to the gym I decided I was nervous. Even if his excuse is real, I had a little crush on him. I wanted this to go well.

I met him in the secluded, smaller area where we always worked. It was equipped with cardio machines and tons of free weights and weight machines, but it was a bit smaller and quieter than the main gym, for people to work with their clients. At 10pm, it was completely deserted.

"Hi Adrienne."

John was waiting for me, leaning against a treadmill. He had some five-o-clock shadow around his jaw.

"Hi," I said meekly, probably letting on how nervous I was.

"I told you if your eating habits didn't improve this week I was going to have to punish you." I looked up and John was suddenly in front of me, looming over me.

"But — I did improve! I did really well this week."

"I know you did, and I knew you would. I just think a little punishment is what you need to be completely on the right track."

It was insane, the things that happened inside me when he said "punishment." It tugged at a place deep inside and I found myself too willing to feel it again to care that this conversation was reckless.

"Okay."

With that, he was on me. He had closed the distance between us and my back was on the trainer's desk and his hips were pressing against me as his mouth found mine. He was a sexy kisser. Way more passionate than I'd expect, but controlled. Rhythmic.

Even so, I couldn't cast my surprise and doubts aside.

I moved away from him. "I don't think we should..." I said the words though I didn't really believe them. This was weird, we were in public. But I wanted it. Like, really wanted it.

"Adrienne," he said sternly, closing the distance between us again, "I think we've established by now that I know what's best for you." He caressed my face with one hand before moving it gently behind my head where it closed, suddenly, on a handful of hair at the back of my head causing me to tilt my head back, exposing my neck. With his other hand on the small of my back he pulled my hips towards his again, so I could feel his erection as he began nibbling at my neck.

I stepped back again, but this time to hop up on the desk and spread my legs so he could move between them, pressing his crotch aggressively against mine as we kissed. I gave in completely to what was about to happen. The thin lining of his gym shorts and my leggings wasn't keeping anything a secret.

He started pressing his hips into mine rhythmically, I think he couldn't help himself. But realizing that I was going to throw caution completely to the wind and embrace this for whatever it was, I wanted to blow him first, to slow everything down for a minute and get my bearings. I slid off the desk and onto my knees in front of him. I looked up — he was smirking again.

His low-hanging gym shorts were no obstacle at all and I simply pulled them down to reveal his erection. I was flattered that he was so hard for me.

"Adrienne," he called from up there, "this is what you do to me." He put one hand on his cock and angled it into my mouth and his other hand on the back of my head, guiding my receipt of it.

I was acutely aware that we were still in a semi-public setting and that this was a rushed and probably ill-advised encounter. But it still seemed innocent, not dirty. We liked each other. Why not give in to what our bodies are telling us?

He was still guiding my blow job, feeding me his cock and then timing his hip thrusts with when he would push on my head and I would bob up and down. Just like how he'd been timing the speed and duration of my runs. I trusted him now. It had been the perfect practice.

I could tell he was really into it by watching his

face and feeling how tense he was down there. After a few minutes he guided me up and I removed my pants completely and laid back on the trainer's desk. He laughed for the first time since I'd met him as he grabbed my thighs and pulled my body into his, entering me.

He thrusted hard as he held my thighs, ensuring I wouldn't bounce too far away. He was the same way he was when he was watching me lift–stoic, measured, controlling. He lifted one hand to caress my face and slipped his thumb into my mouth. I welcomed it and swirled my tongue around it while I sucked, softly. I wanted to show him that I trusted him.

I think this turned him on even more because his speed increased and in turn, I delighted in turning him on and gave into the rhythm of his body on mine. He was going to make me cum. This whole time I'd been so good about not making noise but as I felt that tension roll up from my crotch through my belly and my eyes roll back into my head, I began moaning. He quickly covered my mouth with his hand and lifted me off the desk, holding me in his arms and continuing to thrust into me while I came all over him.

He laid me down again and came quickly after that. As we got dressed again, he dismissed me for the night and I returned home to my first ever personal email from John:

Adrienne,

You've shown a lot of improvement this week. Looking forward to next.

John.

6

Rape Fantasy

I was dating my last boyfriend for four months when he confessed he had a dark fantasy.

We were a fairly new couple so we already couldn't keep our hands off each other. We'd tried a bunch of things just for the hell of it — role play, toys, even some fairly public settings. We'd all but destroyed a bedpost of his antique bed frame with a pair of metal handcuffs.

But he said he wanted more, something he'd never tried before. He was 32 and in his whole sexual career he'd never gotten to explore one thing he was really curious about — he wanted me to resist him, and him to overpower me. A rape fantasy.

If I was honest with myself, the idea turned me on. But I was uncomfortable. What did it mean that this turned him on? That it turned me on? Wasn't that unhealthy, didn't it point to some sort of subconscious misogyny on both of our parts?

But we loved each other and he treated me very well. I knew it couldn't be a sinister request, just something I had to decide if I was okay with. Above all, I was excited that he confided in me something so sensitive and personal, something he'd never felt comfortable enough to share with any other girl.

I googled, "Is it normal if my boyfriend has a rape fantasy?" All the sites said yes. They said it was normal (and yet no one ever brings it up at brunch?) and that it probably doesn't mean anything, just leftover caveman and cavewoman desires. They said to relax, have a safe word, and try it.

So I said yes.

He told me he was happy that I was willing to try something that might be a bit uncomfortable in order to make him happy. It might seem silly that some agreement to try a sex act can reflect a person's character, but it did, he thought, that I was adventurous and that I liked making other people happy.

I wasn't scared of him, he was bigger than me, yes, but in a gentle giant sort of way. He has the human equivalent of what dog trainer's call a "soft mouth" — he just doesn't have it in him to hurt another person, it's not part of his DNA. So we decided on a safe word (Beyoncé) but we both also knew we wouldn't need it. If I looked too afraid or cried or even pleaded too convincingly, he'd stop.

The plan was to pretend I didn't know him. I'd be home, cleaning or cooking or working in some slinky lingerie get up and he'd sneak into the house, like he was a stranger. Then he'd force himself on me.

I spent a lot of time picking out the outfit in question. If the fantasy was going to be somewhat real, I wanted it to be something he'd never seen before, so it would be easier to imagine I was a complete stranger. I didn't want anything slutty, those pieces had their place. I needed something classy and somewhat innocent-looking. At least, as innocent as lingerie could look. I finally settled on a silk negligee I found with long lace sleeves. They made it look almost conservative, like more of my body was covered, when of course, barely anything was covered at all. It barely covered my bottom when I was standing, and when I sat, it rode up to cover only half. It was tight enough that I didn't have to wear a bra with it, and low enough that I couldn't if I wanted to. It was pale pink with black lace, something I'd imagine another girl wearing when she was home alone, waiting for her boyfriend or husband to come home.

To stroke his libido even more, I got a blow out that day. It was big on top, voluminous, but sexy and tousled on bottom. It gave the illusion of being perfectly slept in, like how they must style women's hair for movies after they've slept with someone they shouldn't. I wanted my hair to look a bit different. He didn't have to notice what it was exactly, just that this wasn't the girl he usually came home to.

I painted my nails hot pink too, a color I never wore but which was so striking it would burn into his memory when he saw my fingers wrapped around his cock.

I thought I would feel silly when I was sitting at my desk in this outfit, all made up to pretend I didn't know him. I was worried about letting a giggle slip out, honestly. But when he showed up and grabbed me from behind, there was nothing silly about it. It was all sex — raw desire.

I was seated at my desk when I heard his footsteps, my passion for him (and excitement at this unknown thing I was about to experience) was already bubbling inside me. He didn't announce himself, he simply grabbed my breasts from behind and pulled me up. When I was standing he held me in place with one arm across my body and pulled my hair back with the other, exposing my neck to him.

He kissed me in a very un-him way. It was needy and brutal, I would have bruises there tomorrow and there was no questioning it, I was just going to have to be okay with it. It was completely out of my control.

He was more aggressive than I ever knew him to be. He'd thrown me down on the bed once or twice but this time he didn't stop to ask if I was okay. He didn't laugh, didn't stop to give me little pecks. He glared at me, holding his face over mine, forcibly tilting my head up so that I met his gaze. He wanted to watch me react to him.

His hands were all over me in a way they hadn't been since we first started hooking up. They were greedy, devouring every surface, pinching, pulling, grabbing, scratching. And even though this was strange, even though he gave off the aura of a strange man in this moment my legs opened to him and I knew my body wanted nothing more than for him to climb on top of me and be inside me.

Remembering the fantasy, I mitigated my exclamations of pleasure with whimpering some "no's" and "stop's." This excited him. I could tell because his hands moved faster, rougher.

He quickly pulled my panties off without even looking at them and extended his middle finger inside me while his face hovered just above mine, watching as my mouth opened in response to his movements and my eyes rolled back into my head.

I brushed his hands off my body. I squirmed. I made him remember that I was not a docile female, a weakling at his disposal.

He became rougher. He held my hands over my head with just one of his large hands and used the other to unbuckle his belt and pull his pants down haphazardly.

"Lie still you little slut."

I'd never heard him speak this way. I was shocked into submission and nearly oblivious to him entering me. He was so turned on, he was letting himself be completely uncensored.

He began to slam into me, the kind of jackhammer sex he was usually too good for, but which was hot, under the circumstances. It was rushed and unfamiliar and all about whatever he wanted. He was using my body exactly how he desired. His grunts and moans were louder and more fervent than I was used to, a reward for indulging him.

After only a few minutes, I could tell he was getting close. Without warning, he pulled out and ejaculated all over my new, expensive lingerie. I laid there as he left, waiting until I'd showered before he returned, my familiar, loving boyfriend again, gushing with compliments about the sex we'd just had.

7

Sex with My Boyfriend Whenever He Wanted it

It started with porn. We watched porn together sometimes, more his desire than mine, but whatever, it was kind of hot. I mean, porn is weird and unsexy and a bit depressing if you think about it too much or pay a lot of attention to it, but if you can find a good one and pay attention for the beginning only, it can be good. It's like watching a horror movie and you tense up and your blood pressure rises even though you know it's fake —

given the stimuli, your body can't help but produce a physical reaction.

Anyways, we watched porn together sometimes and I knew he watched it alone. I'm not like, "the cool girl" who's totally okay with her boyfriend watching porn but I knew it was an uphill battle and one that wasn't going to end well for either of us, so I tried to use it to bring us closer together. One night, loosened up by a few stiff drinks over ice we drank on his balcony, watching the city lights come on and turn off — the full metropolitan life cycle in one night — I asked him what he liked about porn, and whether access to me or all the other women in the world (hotter ones, I even gave him) would be better, ideally.

His answer surprised me, it wasn't about quality or quantity, but about availability. With me, (and he loved me very much, he clarified), he had to woo me, constantly. Sex was never a given, and this is a biological difference between men and women. He was trying, all the time to make me think of him sexually and to initiate sex and even my higher-than-average female libido couldn't keep up with him. As loving and as open and assuring as I was towards him, he was still getting rejected by me in this way, often (and even more often if he would be honest about how frequently he wanted sex).

And so watching porn made sense to me in a way it never had before. The fantasy, the real fantasy, was a world free of rejection, from the tired trope of the guy who wants sex more than his girlfriend does. I felt bad about it, to be honest, as much as I loved him, why did he have to suffer these feelings that he was somehow not enough?

By personality, I am a maximizer. I am the kind of girl with checkmarks and to-do lists and the one who breaks her New Year's resolutions into "action items." So I took this sort-of imbalance in our sex life as a challenge — what kind of system could we get on that would work for both of us?

The very first thing to do was to switch places. If our sex life was currently running solely on Adrienne-time we needed to switch it to Boyfriend-time, at least to try it and see what it was like. So we decided that for one week, we would do just that. We would be running our relationship on his biological frequency instead of mine. I could try anything for a week. Boyfriend was too cautious to be excited, as if I would change my mind if he showed too much enthusiasm.

We started on Monday with morning sex before he left for work. I was in the habit of spending the night at his place (it was nicer than mine, albeit less homey — and I'm a writer so I don't have to get up and get dressed at the crack of dawn like he does) and usually he lets me sleep and I talk to him dreamily while he gets ready, without really waking up. But today was the first day of Sex-On-His-Terms week and I woke up to his breath on my neck and his hand running up my leg, grazing the boy-cut panties I wore to bed. He was ready to start.

I opened my legs to him immediately. There was something freeing about the choice already being made. I was going to have sex with him, I was necessarily "in the mood" because I'd already decided I was going to be. For an overly-analytical maximizer like me, decisions are a lot of work, and knowing this one was already made felt relaxing and luxurious. Like morning sex. I made him 45 minutes late that day. He blamed it on a faulty alarm clock.

I napped afterwards and woke up to several text messages from him, rare for having just seen him off a few hours ago.

This morning was so hot. I can't wait for more.

The second was more forceful than complimentary:

Stay in bed. I'm coming home for lunch.

I laughed. This was part of a fantasy he had about my schedule. When we first started dating he thought that a freelance schedule meant that I would always be available to him. He talked about lunchtime rendezvous — coming home to pillage me and then leaving me there naked while he returned to work. I filled him in on the reality of deadlines and the hours of uninterrupted focus it took to produce something really good. He got it, but it was like telling a kid Santa isn't real. Today was going to be his redemption.

I have to admit, it was hot to snuggle back into his linens, smelling him, waiting for his return — to be instructed not to dress. It was the kind of thing where I might usually touch myself and think of his hands instead of mine, but his return was coming so soon that I didn't, I just waited for him and smiled my cat-who-got-the-mouse smile when he walked in, already unbuckling his belt. I was wet for him, more than usual — it was all the waiting. He felt like a stud, I could tell, as I crawled across the bed towards him, still naked from the morning sex, and climbed on top of him. I rode him without even unbuttoning his pale blue work shirt. I wondered if it would smell like me for the rest of the day.

I didn't go home after he returned to work. Usually I would have let myself out long ago, gone home and showered and have several hours of work at the corner coffee shop under my belt. I used his shower and didn't bother dressing, simply draping his t-shirt over me while I helped myself to his much fancier computer. I had to save time somewhere, and he was probably just going to undress me again when he got home anyway. (He did.)

Tuesday morning I told him I was going to go home and work, and that I would make dinner for him that night if he wanted to come over. I wanted to keep going with my promise, but I also needed to get some work done so I figured the added promise of a home cooked meal would be enough to tide him over through the day. I made a lasagna so I would have plenty of time to get ready after I was done cooking. I showered and sprayed perfume in all his favorite places. I dressed in lingerie instead of clothes and then when he texted me that he was leaving work, I tried something silly I'd read in Cosmo once. I was kind of sexed out and I needed to get back in the mood so I put on some relaxing music and laid in bed. Without trying to get off or do anything other than relax, I placed my vibrator inside me and thought about him — again, nothing too intense, just kind of opening myself up for the evening. As robotic and forced as the action seemed at first, when I put it away and got up to pour wine for dinner, I was in an entirely different mood. I wasn't tired anymore, I was desirous, the knock at the door was one of promise instead of obligation.

I kissed him, open-mouth, in the stairwell, surprising even myself with my unwillingness to even walk up the stairs before I touched him. I was already ready, already wanting him and he, in turn, was turned on by my suddenly elevated interest. I wanted to feel his weight on me, and I placed my hands on his lower back, pulling him into me and feeling his jeans rub against the thin fabric of my negligee. I turned, finally, to lead him up the stairs to my kitchen and felt his hands lift the back of the slip and grab my ass fully in his hands. I almost couldn't keep walking, the needing-him sensation inside me about doubled with that touch. While we ate, his hands never stopped touching me — rubbing my thigh, pulling me into him by wrapping his arm around my shoulder, brushing my hair back from my face. It was, oddly, an extremely romantic meal we both prolonged, because the tension building between us was so fun to play with. Every touch was becoming unbearable.

After dinner we didn't go to the couch or pretend we were going to do an activity for a bit. We went to my bedroom. We kissed like we hadn't kissed in forever — long, deep, high-school kisses. He walked me back to my bed and laid me down beneath him, kissing my collarbone and murmuring sweet nothings between breaths. He slid a finger inside me and held his face above mine, watching my reaction, cherishing my reaction. He told me I was beautiful, that he loved watching me respond to him.

His confidence at this point was intoxicating. He knew I was on board with whatever he wanted to do and instead of it turning him into a greedy tyrant, it relaxed him, it opened him up. I felt closer to him than ever before.

When he pulled me to the edge of the bed and entered me, it was slower and more lust-filled than usual. This wasn't get-it-over-with sex. This was vacation sex on a Tuesday night. He took a pillow and I obligingly lifted my hips so he could place it underneath them and return to pushing himself into me, deeper now. He placed his forearms next to my arms as he leaned over me, maximizing our skin-to-skin contact.

Convinced now that this sex session would be leisurely, he pulled out of me and bent down, flicked his tongue over my clit as my eyes rolled back into my head and I squirmed before him. I wondered if he could taste himself in me?

His finger was inside me again, swirling around, feeling the width of me while he kissed and flicked me on the outside. He stimulated me all at once, like an expert. Every erogenous zone was on fire. I heard myself begging him to fuck before I realized that was even what I wanted — and he was on top of me again, thrusting into me like I asked, like I needed, filling me, driving me over the edge.

For once, I came before he did — in a hot, sticky, dizzy wave that came roaring out of me.

He came next, catapulted into it by me spasming around his dick. I felt his heat inside me and his breathing slow, finally. Lying supine next to my breathless match, I couldn't believe there were five more days of this.

8

My Boss Bent Me Over his Desk

Every morning I would get myself ready for work — find a dress that looked professional but also clung nicely to my curves, apply makeup, curl my hair, and spritz a small amount of slightly too sexy for work fragrance on the nape of my neck. I always wore heels so that I could be closer to his 6'4 frame. And then I'd arrive at my desk and try to do as much work as possible before my distraction arrived.

I started working at a large real estate company as a records clerk a few months ago. It wasn't the work I imagined I'd be doing with my English degree but I'd graduated months ago and my job search had been very frustrating and unsuccessful, so I felt lucky to have a decent paying full time gig, even if it was nowhere near my dream. And the perks... well, that would be the 30-year-old CEO, Jack Singer.

At first I thought I was imagining it–this handsome, impossibly successful man couldn't possibly be interested in me. But his eyes lingered too long, and he trailed his fingers along my back when no one else was around. He found excuses for us to work late, alone together, and always ordered in a complicated dinner, so we'd be at the table in his office for quite a long time, just talking. Nothing had really happened yet, but it was only a matter of time. I was completely in lust with him, with his dark hair and eyes, his broad shoulders, with the way he talked about struggling to fit into his new lifestyle because he still felt like a kid from a working class family playing pretend.

And so I fell into a routine of mostly being enamored and distracted. Today, like most days he walked in and greeted me. His knowing smile elicited a familiar tug between my legs that floated up through my stomach. I wanted him.

As my attraction grew, my dresses got shorter and tighter. I was waiting for him to make the first move, but I couldn't wait much longer. Today, in particular, was a creation I shouldn't have purchased on my salary, but I was fairly certain it was going to do the trick. It was a long-sleeved red sweater dress that hugged my curves but was loose enough to allow it to be short without looking obscene. I'd paired it with black high-heeled boots that hit just above the knee. It was the kind of outfit that would make a quick encounter very easy...which is what I spent most of my time fantasizing about.

Jack walked in the door looking as attractive as ever, he hadn't shaved this morning and the dark stubble accentuated his square jaw.

"Good morning Adrienne," he called, locking eyes with me and smirking, as his gaze traveled down my body to my thighs, exposed between my sweater dress and boots.

My mouth hung open a bit in delight as I smiled back at him. "It is a good morning."

I don't know how he had even made it into his

office to turn on his computer when I got an email from him:

> Adrienne,
>
> I'm going to need you to stay late tonight and pull some records so I can prepare for the DRC meeting tomorrow.
>
> -JS

I couldn't stop the smile that spread throughout my entire body. This is it.

I'm sure it's not the best idea in the world to start sleeping with your boss. But I couldn't remember ever having such a strong physical and mental connection with someone, and I trusted him, he was going to act responsibly for both of us, if something bad happened and things weren't great, he could help me get a similar job somewhere else. I didn't want to say no to something so intoxicating for a job I cared very little about.

The day flew by because all I did was daydream about various fantasies I wanted to recreate with Mr. Singer. As people started to leave for the day, I was confused to see him, too, in his overcoat. "Adrienne, I'm sorry, you'll have to pull the files without me, I've got a last minute dinner I need to attend."

I couldn't hide the disappointment in my face, I'm sure he caught it, but I didn't really care. I was all wound up... for nothing.

"Sure thing."

The minute he left I called a delivery service and ordered a bottle of wine. I may have to stay late and work alone, but I could at least enjoy myself.

Well, one glass turned into three and by the time I'd carefully organized and laid out all the files Jack would need on the table in his office, I was buzzed enough to make a very bad decision. What a shame, I thought, trailing my fingers along the edge of his desk, this is the perfect height.

I sat down in Jack's expensive leather office chair for a moment, to rest a moment before I went home. I could see why he liked this chair, it made me feel powerful. Sitting behind his desk made me feel powerful. Jack's smirk this morning made me feel even more powerful, I thought, and remembering the way his face looked as he stared at my legs made me feel excited all over again. I felt the same tug between my legs.

Carelessly I sat back and closed my eyes, running

my hand up my thigh, pretending it was his large, masculine hand. I began rubbing higher, brushing the barrier of the black lace underwear I'd put on this morning, with high hopes for how it would be used. I could feel how damp they were, it had been a long day of build up and no release.

I deserved to be be a little reckless.

I reached my hand inside my panties and placed one leg on Jack's desk. His view would be excellent if he had bothered to stay. I leaned back as I began to slowly finger my clit. It was so relaxing to think about Jack doing this, so perfect.

"Ahem."

I jerked forward, closing my legs and removing my hands from between them in one quick moment. Jack was standing in front of me. Oh shit, I thought before my tipsy brain realized he didn't look angry. He was smirking.

"I'm sorry, to interrupt, but you realize you're using my office right now?"

"I'm so sorry, sir," I said, the alcohol giving me the courage to emphasize the last word.

"Sir' now, is it?" He asked, moving next to me, standing above me looking down with that look on his face.

"It's whatever you want it to be."

He reached forward and caressed my throat with one hand, I stood frozen in my seat. His seat. He held my face in his hands, silently thinking for a long minute. He continued to rub my neck with one of his hands while the other traveled to my crotch where he felt how wet I was. "Good girl."

That snapped me out of my stupor and I grabbed his hips and pulled him closer. He smirked again as I unbuckled his pants and found a full on erection waiting for me.

"I've been waiting to do this for a long time," I said, as I licked him from the shaft of his penis to the tip, watching his face react the whole time.

"You're not the only one," he replied, his hands now stroking my hair.

But I didn't just want to tell him how much I wanted him, I wanted to show him. I took all of his cock into my mouth and felt the familiar adjustment my throat made to accept it. I used to think this would make me gag, but practice told me it actually supplied more liquid from the back of my throat, making the whole process easier, and more pleasurable for him. The hand that suddenly tightened around my hair confirmed this.

"Get up," he said, hurriedly lifting me up and spinning me around. He grabbed my breasts roughly, bending me forward over the desk. My only thought was, Yessss.

He lifted the small amount of material covering my butt and entered me from behind. His cock was perfect. It filled me on all sides, but it didn't hurt. He thrust into me roughly, but rhythmically.

"You've been a very good employee, I thought it was time I give you a reward," Jack said, his voice lower, hoarser than usual. With that, he gave my ass a hard smack. I screamed in surprise and he chuckled. This was even hotter than I imagined.

He began thrusting harder, using one hand to position my hips and the other to massage my breast, occasionally pinching the nipple. I told him I was about to cum and he moved his hand down to my pussy to finger my clit and guide me along. I felt his muscles tense up at the same time as mine. I couldn't keep my voice down as pleasure took over my body, as my eyes rolled back into my head, as I felt him cum and collapse on top of my back.

We laid there for a moment before he spoke.

"Adrienne, I'm going to need you to work late every night this week."

9

Skirts

It had been a long weekend since I slept with my boss — since he caught me in a very compromising position and finished the act himself — but I was still surprised that I hadn't heard from him right away afterward.

I'm not sure what I expected, flowers on my desk, a proclamation of love, a promotion (?), a wink as he walked by? This was all new territory for me.

I'd woken in a daze before my alarm even went off. I remembered the events of the previous week,

Jack coming in to his office where I was supposed to be working late and instead catching me at his desk, touching myself and envisioning his masculine hand between my legs instead of my own. He'd seemed pleasantly surprised, right? Why was my phone silent? Why was there no word from him?

I was already worrying as I picked out my outfit — a snug black pencil skirt, a semi-sheer black top, black nylons, and black stilettos. I was at least going to look confident if I couldn't act that way.

When I got to the office I saw Jack's door was still closed, nothing unusual, I always arrived before him. I sat at my desk outside his office and tried to busy myself, or at least look like I was busy, while I kept watch out of the corner of my eye for him to appear. Nothing.

At lunch I asked our small company's operations director if he'd be in that day — she was a loopy older lady but she always knew everything that was going on in the office. "Didn't you hear," she said, with a genuine look of surprise on her face, "Jack's traveling. Last minute trip for the DRI client. He sent an email out this morning." My heart sank again, I hadn't gotten the email, and he always cced me on stuff like that. Maybe he was unhappy about what happened. Something was up.

Back at my desk I racked my brain for a manufactured reason to contact him. I had to see what his tone would be like in the response. Finally, I just went with something that seemed even remotely plausible:

> Hi Jack–
>
> I heard you had to travel today last minute. Do you need me to take care of anything here at the office?
>
> -Adrienne

And then I waited impatiently for a reply to appear in my inbox. Several hours of hitting refresh later:

> Adrienne–
>
> Thanks for working late last night, I have everything I need for the meeting. We'll speak tomorrow.
>
> -Jack

As I finished reading, I felt my phone buzz on my desk. It was a text from Jack, "PS wear a skirt."

Jesus.

Okay. Everything was fine. More than fine. That was a flirtatious text. He didn't regret following his impulse, bending me over his desk. He wanted more. Good. So did I.

Jack was always a weird combination of mysterious and forthright. He was blunt and honest whenever I asked him about something, but he never shared without prodding. It intrigued me, or at least made me feel flattered that I was getting to be privy to his private side. And I'd find out even more soon.

I spent the rest of the afternoon online shopping for the perfect short-but-not-too-short skirt to wear the next day and fantasizing about having his hands on me again. The sex we'd had was primal, passionate — I wasn't sure how it could get any better but I'd be thrilled with more of the same. I drove to the mall after work to try on a few of the more promising skirts, the sensation of pulling them on and off felt heightened, I was very aware of everything touching my skin. Luckily, I found the perfect almost knee-length but flouncy black skirt I could wear with a thin sweater tucked into it. This would be totally hard to resist.

Feeling emboldened by Jack's text, I couldn't help but be flirtatious, it was hard to say no to myself with how wound-up I was feeling inside. I snapped a photo of the skirt in the dressing room mirror and texted it to Jack. I expected no response, or at least I must have not expected a response because I was surprised when I heard my phone buzz a few minutes later.

It was Jack:

"Shorter."

I gasped out loud in the cashier line and then exited it to purchase another skirt I'd tried on — the one I thought was probably inappropriate for work. I didn't care if it was inappropriate for work, the job didn't mean much to me and I was so shocked by Jack responding with anything other than a compliment, it just wasn't how most men acted. I wanted to please him enough to learn more.

In the morning, as I pulled on my new skirt and straightened the shirt I was wearing with it I felt more nervous than I could remember being. This was a dumb sex thing with my boss, sure, it was probably irresponsible, but I was responsible in more than enough other areas of my life to make up for it. I wouldn't be at this job long, I may as well have fun here. And I'd never experienced something so intoxicating as the way Jack had handled me. The roughness of his touch coupled with the pleasure in his eyes and in his voice.

When I got to work I was surprised to see Jack's door was open, he was early. With trepidation and a kind of butterfly feeling that extended downward from my stomach, I knocked on the door and peeked in, "Jack?"

"Good morning Adrienne."

He was sitting at his desk, reclining. He looked very sexy like that, both playful and poised.

"I see you follow instructions well," he said, his eyes glued to my legs — quite a bit of which were uncovered by the skirt I'd decided on.

"Only for you sir." I laughed as I said it.

It wasn't funny but the intensity of the situation made me giggle. I wasn't used to being so serious. I walked to his desk and perched myself on the edge of it, trying my best to look sophisticated. He placed one hand on my bare thigh rubbing it, dangerously high. I glanced back at the open door, no one was due in for a bit longer, but what if someone came in early? Shouldn't we shut it? And yet... I could also feel my worries being drowned out by another voice inside me that was praying his hand would keep moving.

"Not now Adrienne. I just want a peek of what I'm going to find later."

He pulled me off the desk and into a standing position in front of him and moved his hand farther up until I could see a look of pleasant surprise cross his face as he realized I wasn't wearing panties. He bit his lip.

Feeling awkward about just standing there while he touched me, I leaned forward to kiss him. He turned his head so that he could whisper in my ear, "Good girl Adrienne." Then he kissed my earlobe and continued down my neck, one of his fingers now inside me making strong, circular motions. I gripped his chair for balance as keeping upright on my own was becoming increasingly difficult. I couldn't think with what he was doing to me.

He pulled his hand out of me and placed it on the back of my thigh. I could feel some of my wetness smearing down my leg and I wasn't sure if he'd intended that or not, but it was hot.

"Mmm. I'm going to bend you over my desk later. After I'm finished with my lunch call." It was a statement, not a request — and he was right about that, there was no way I was saying no. He looked at me and I nodded, pulling my skirt down as far as it would go. I turned to leave his office until the appointed time and was dismissed with a playful slap on the back of my skirt.

I returned to my desk and waited to be summoned.

10

My Boss Made Me Strip for Him

My boss and I had gotten into a routine over the last few weeks: I would wear short skirts to work and try to pass the time "working" from my desk outside his office. Really though, I was texting him dirty things and we'd chat back and forth until we couldn't take it any longer — at which point he'd summon me into his office ("Adrienne, I need you to step in here for a moment for a conference call") and bend me over his desk. It never took more than a few minutes, we were both so wound up by the time we actually touched each other.

My days were always a blur, everything was so exciting, I was lost in fantasy — or else living it out — every minute. I was always either revving up or winding down — building anticipation or releasing it. When I woke up, I couldn't wait to go to work. Life was fucking great.

My boss, Jack, seemed to be enjoying himself too. At least, if his near-constant erections were any indication.

Today I'd outdone myself in preparation: brand new thigh highs that were hidden underneath my dress, the lacy tops of which ended just a few inches below the tippy tops of my legs. I thought he'd appreciate how they made me seem dressed, even while undressed. In the semi-privacy of the area under my desk I pulled my dress up a bit and snapped a pic of the thigh highs and texted it to Jack. There, let him try to work with that on his mind.

I went to the break room to get a glass of water and sure enough, when I returned Jack was calling me. "Adrienne? Is that you? Can you come in here for a sec?"

Gleefully I set my water down and practically

skipped into his office. I shut the door behind me and turned. That's when I noticed things were off.

Nate, our 41-year-old human resources director was seated across from Jack at the table in his office. "Have a seat Adrienne," he said as my heart quickly sank to the very bottom of my chest, "we have something to discuss."

He knew.

That was all I could think, over and over. Jack owned the company — would it matter if we were being bad? It must or we wouldn't be having this meeting at all. Maybe he wanted to put an end to it and he chose the most bizarre method imaginable?

Nate cleared his throat and dropped the bomb, "Adrienne, we've had some complaints from the staff about your wardrobe. The length of your skirts is simply not professional."

I looked at Jack, trying to see how he wanted me to respond. I was only wearing such short skirts by his request!

"Umm, I'm so sorry." I started. This was actually humiliating. I was going to throw up. Or cry. But I needed to get through this conversation first. "I had no idea, I just thought that was... um, like the style now. I won't wear them anymore."

I was trying my hardest to not react, to be monotone, to not be the emotional girl who cries at work — to moderate success. My voice was cracking a bit but I think my expression was blank.

Nate looked really uncomfortable. I searched Jack's face for his reaction. He finally spoke, "Adrienne... I think this is a bit silly. But we can't have you making people uncomfortable and interfering with their productivity. Since Nate isn't in the office every day I've volunteered to be the neutral party here. I'll be enforcing your promise to dress in a way that is consistent with the professional values of this office."

There it was.

The right corner of his mouth twitched upwards. He was enjoying this! It was so infuriating. I was extremely stressed out, mustering all my internal strength to simply not cry and he was fantasizing about chasing me around the office with a ruler to measure the length of my skirts. I promised Nate, again, to be extremely conscious of my clothing, thanked them both, and dismissed myself. I grabbed my purse and took an early, unannounced lunch. I needed to clear my head.

When I returned, it was to a post-it on my desk from Jack.

Let's meet offsite tonight. Filio's. 8pm.

There was no way to answer yes or no, his door was shut, he was gone for the rest of the day. Though, frankly, even given the sobering discussion I'd just had, I was excited to take our fling out of the office. He was taking me to dinner. This was a welcome change of pace.

When I arrived at dinner, I couldn't hold myself in. "I can't believe you were smirking while I was getting in trouble!" It was the first time I'd ever raised my voice to him. "I was only wearing those skirts because YOU asked me to!"

He laughed as if this was some hysterical joke. And, honestly, it was pretty funny. Like your parents catching you make out with a guy outside the middle school dance.

"I am going to enjoy measuring your skirts, however." He looked devilish. Of course he was, he was getting off scot-free.

"You know it only makes me want you when you talk like that." I didn't want to stay mad at him, and the whole thing seemed silly now that we were out of the office. "But maybe we do need to keep it out of the office?"

"I have no interest in doing that," Jack said, his tone matter of fact. "I feel more invigorated in my work than I have in a long time." Now he looked vulnerable, like he was admitting something that made him uncomfortable. He was letting me in, if just a tiny bit. He realized this at the same time I did, as he sounded a bit harder when he continued. "You will have to choose. Tomorrow I will measure your skirt and if it's not short enough for me I will punish you. Of course, as your boss I'm going to have to encourage you to follow human resources suggestions... so it appears as if you're stuck."

I swallowed. The way he hung on that phrase, *I'm going to have to punish you.* I couldn't help myself from writhing a bit in my chair, the promise of this idea tugged at me between my legs. I had no intention of following Jack's orders. I needed to see what his punishment would consist of.

"We'll have to see tomorrow," I said as coyly as I could. I tried to act sexy around him, but I was so enthralled I had no idea if it worked. At least now I had a hint he felt the same way. He winked and my body doubled down on the familiar pang of lust below my abdomen.

In the morning, I put on one of my old outfits. I wasn't going to stoop so low as to wear pants, but this dress hit just below the knee when I was standing. The old ladies in the office would have nothing to complain about. But Jack would...

I was standing in the hallway when he arrived, putting away some files he'd used the previous day. He eyed me with a mixture of disapproval and excitement. I knew what was coming.

Sure enough, a few minutes after I got back to my desk, I heard his familiar call, "Adrienne, can you come in here?" Excited, I walked into his office.

"Shut the door behind you."

He was standing in front of his desk, leaning back on it with his arms crossed. He had that far-off look of concentration he had when I was pleasuring him. I loved that look.

"Tsk Tsk. Your skirt is far too long. Come here so I can check." I obliged, approaching him. He pulled at the fabric and made an exaggerated noise of disgust. "The fabric is so thick! It leaves far too much to my imagination. And you know what happens when we leave things to my imagination."

I quivered. I couldn't help it. His calmness — the way he controlled the whole situation. It made me drunk on him.

"Um, yes I do know what happens?" I wasn't sure how he wanted me to respond.

"Show me what I'm missing out on."

I lifted my skirt in the front, enough to reveal the lacy thong I was wearing underneath.

"Let me see the back."

I turned and allowed him to see my bare butt. Even though we'd had sex in his office many times, we always kept our clothes mostly on. I was more nervous now. He was just standing there, examining me. I felt very exposed.

"Strip for me."

He wanted me completely naked? I didn't love that idea... his office was brightly lit and we weren't in the throes of passion or anything. I'd just be standing there, all my flaws out in the open.

"Adrienne, don't hesitate. I'm already displeased with you."

I grinned. For some reason when he expressed displeasure it didn't come across as disrespectful, but of caring enough about me to know I wanted to turn him on. I pulled my sweater over my head and unzipped my skirt before stepping out of it.

"Bra and panties, too."

I removed them. The sensation of standing before him completely naked while he was fully clothed was surprisingly intoxicating. I moved toward him, I needed him now.

"I want you to get on your knees and tell me why I should fuck you when you won't even wear your lovely skirts for me."

I obliged. "Please Jack. I'm sorry. I had to. The women in the office — they'd complain to Nate again if I didn't change."

"And who do you care about pleasing?"

"You."

"That's right. Now come here."

He took me and bent me over his desk (finally, I thought) but it wasn't for the reason I'd hoped. He spanked me. Hard. Methodically. Rubbing my ass in between slaps, savoring it.

"Jack," I breathed. I couldn't handle this anymore. "Can you please fuck me now? I'm so turned on."

"And you think you deserve it now?" He still sounded stern.

"Pleeease." It was all I could get out. I was writhing on his desk.

"You might not yet, but I'll indulge you this once."

I heard him unzip his pants and I paused to spread my legs out, providing him easy access. He entered me quickly, without easing into it and thrusted hard right away, pressing me into his desk. I felt his hands grab my hips and pull me back into him, quickly.

"Mmm, you feel so fucking good." He was losing himself, I could tell. He groaned as he fucked me. The build-up had been inside him, too.

"Cum inside me, please." I begged him. It wasn't a fetish I was into, or something I'd even thought about before that moment. But I wanted it and the volume of his groan in response solidified that it was a mutual desire.

With a few final pumps he emptied himself into me and pulled out. I lay breathless on his desk, too wasted to move. He handed me my clothes, "Maybe you'll think more wisely about your wardrobe choices tomorrow."

11

Dinner Party

It should be known that my boyfriend is not a "controversial sex fantasy" kind of guy. He's a "good guy" (and maybe all "good guys" are also "controversial sex fantasy" kind of guys, I don't know), he's the one you bring home to your parents and you don't even pump up in the car ride there because you know, without fail, he's going to make a good impression. Jake is affable, responsible and loyal. I always felt safe with him, which was why I was pressing him to hear about his deep, dark, sexual desires.

I knew, whatever they were, I'd feel comfortable enough with him that we could try it.

I remember the first time I met Richard, Jake's boss, at last year's Christmas party. He was younger than I thought he would be. In his early 40s with a great body, perfectly styled hair with just a hint of grey. We hit it off immediately. He was intimidating, but easy to like. I could see why Jake looked up to him.

They had met in grad school when Richard consulted on Jake's thesis. They clicked and he's been sort of a mentor to Jake ever since, that's actually what made him come to New York, to work with Richard. We had long since started our life together, and Richard was a welcome part of it. He and his wife had come over for a lot of intimate dinner parties that turned into very late nights over opened bottles of Chianti.

One night while I was clearing the dishes in the sink and Richard was still sitting in the living room. Jake came up from behind me and nuzzled my neck, wrapping his arms around me like he always does, pressing his hips into me in a way that made me glad it was almost time for us to be alone.

"Tonight's going really well, don't you think?" he asked me.

"Yeah, babe. Of course."

Kathryn, Richard's wife, was MIA for the evening. Down with a flu or cold of some sort. Richard seemed glad to be away for the night.

"Do you ever think about Richard?... Do you find him attractive?" Jake had pulled away from behind me and we were now facing each other.

I sort of laughed and said, "Well...yeah. Sure. He's a very attractive man." That's the thing about Jake. I knew I could be totally honest with him.

And truthfully, I had thought about Richard. What young woman doesn't fantasize about the powerful, confident, worldly man in her life? He was like a younger, fitter Javier Bardem. A girl could do worse.

"Yeah, I think he's sexy, honestly," I told Jake. "Distinguished, like you'll be one day."

"Interesting," Jake said with a smirk on his face. "That's really interesting."

"Why do you ask? You jealous?" I teased.

"Not at all actually. I think it's kind of hot."

"It's hot that I have a crush on your boss?"

He leaned into me, his 5 o'clock shadow

scratching me as he breathed into my neck, "Remember when you asked me if I had any special fantasies?"

And then I knew where he was going with this, and I thought my immediate reaction would be hurt — that he was okay with me having sex with another guy — but it wasn't. It was an overwhelming feeling of being turned on, of immediate wanting. Jake was saying that not only was my little crush okay, that it turned him on to think about his boss and I being together.

"I want Richard to fuck you. And I want to watch."

He knew it turned me on when he talked like this, when he took charge. I always felt like that made me his. And, honestly, it was kinda sweet that he wanted to get his friend laid.

I looked at him and smiled. "Okay," I said. "I'm down."

As I turned around and headed towards the living room Jake slapped me on my ass. "Good girl."

Richard was sitting on the couch finishing a glass of wine when we came back in the room. He had put on some light music.

I rolled my eyes a bit, he must have known this was going to happen. They'd cooked up this scheme over after-work drinks, to be sure. The idea excited me, that they'd spent a few hours over scotches talking about me, trying to figure out how to get Richard in my pants.

It made me feel a bit braver about the whole thing, I wasn't going to make an idiot out of myself. I sat next to Richard and immediately propped my legs up in his lap and cozied into him. I went to the old standby, the thing men love talking about (how much of a martyr they are). "Jake's been telling me how hard you've been working, poor thing."

It worked, he launched into a story about ball-buster clients and late nights at the office. I rubbed the scruff on the back of his head while he talked, goading him into telling me more, into opening up to me, but never going too far, letting him think he was the one seducing me.

As he talked about work he rested his arm on my leg, rubbing it nonchalantly while talking, as if the whole thing was totally normal. I looked over, interested in Jake's reaction. He made eye contact with me and winked. This was exactly what he wanted but I knew he wouldn't be satisfied until one of us made a real move.

I shifted my legs in his lap, making sure one of them ran over his cock (I could feel it now) and that the movement shifted my dress up, so my pink lace panties were now visible to him. His eyes moved from my legs to my panties to my lips, and I smiled.

In a movement so quick I didn't immediately register what was happening, Richard had pulled me on top of him, slid his hands into my panties, and wrapped his lips around my neck, kissing me greedily. I gasped into his ear as I felt his hands (sadly more expertly than Jakes) stimulate all the right places inside of me.

I lifted my head and kissed Richard full on on the mouth. He tasted like wine and like peppermint, as if he'd popped one when we were in the other room, in preparation. I thought of all the times I'd seen him and thought about what a sexy older man he was and now this was finally happening, and with Jake's blessing!

Richard pulled my panties down and slid his cock deep inside me. He was larger than I anticipated and much larger than Jake, so I let out a surprised moan.

"Jake is a very good employee," Richard said, his voice lower and hoarser than usual. "I'll make sure he gets an extra bonus this year for letting me fuck his girl."

I looked over at Jake, he looked barely able to control himself. Richard was laying over me, fucking me, staring at me as if he couldn't believe his luck. I felt like a goddess. While he fucked me he pulled the hand that had been inside me up over my face. Obligingly I opened my mouth and tasted myself on him, swirling my tongue over each of his fingers.

His speed increased, he was losing it. "I'm going to cum inside your girlfriend," he announced to Jake. I felt myself tightening around Richard, so full of pleasure — not only from his cock and the skill with which he laid into me but from the forbidden feeling of fucking my boyfriend's boss in front of him, of doing something so deliciously bad.

When he came, I felt it deep inside me. I loved it. I was desired not only by my hot, good boyfriend but by his incredibly sexy boss as well.

After Richard left, Jake and I retreated to our bedroom, laying naked on the sheets in silence for a moment. Oh fuck, I thought. What would happen now? Would our relationship be able to handle what just happened? Would Jake regret this night?

"Babe, come here," Jake pulled me closer to him. "You're fucking incredible. Do you realize that?"

"This was exactly what you wanted? You're not going to regret this tomorrow? It's not going to jeopardize anything at work will it?" I knew Jake had enjoyed himself in the moment but I needed to know everything would be okay, that we would be okay.

He kissed me on my forehead and laughed. "No. If anything, this just made work a whole lot better."

12

He Came Home with a Vibrator

One night he bought me a vibrator and brought it to me in a nicely wrapped package.

"I'm going to tell you what to do with this," he instructed. "Take your clothes off, slut."

Addressing me this way always looped a pang of lust through my body that originated, whether physically or psychologically, between my legs and floats upward, like heat. I removed my yoga pants and took my shirt off, ensuring my breasts did a little bounce when I removed my bra, for his benefit. I'd dressed for this, for quick removal.

"Lay on the bed and put the vibrator on your clit. Do not put it inside you."

I spread my legs for him and turned the vibe on, holding it against myself. The effect was immediate. My breath became deliberate, inhaling and exhaling lust. More, I needed more.

I wanted his hands on me, in me. I'm one of the few women who thinks fingering is vastly underrated and all I wanted to complement the steady buzz on my clit were his thick fingers inside me, making me squirm beneath him.

"Can I have you?" I asked this and it sounded disjointed as it came out, I was getting sex drunk already.

"I want you inside me," I tried again. Clitoral stimulation is great and it gets you off but what woman doesn't prefer her man's cock inside her, filling her, slippery, hitting all the right spots?

"Keep going," was his only response. His face was serious and intent. He watched my expression as I tried to think straight, as I tried to convince him to fuck me.

The vibrator felt amazing but I wanted him. I needed him.

"Please. Please baby, I need your cock inside me.

I need you to fuck me. I need you to fuck me so bad."

"Show me." He was still instructing but his tone was softer. "You look beautiful right now."

He pushed two fingers into my mouth and I opened up and lifted my head to welcome them. The only thing my head was saying was to do it. Anything to please him, anything to get him to fuck me.

He pushed them deeper into my mouth. "Show me what you want."

I closed my lips around his fingers and ran my tongue up and down them recoiling slightly as this movement grazed the back of my mouth.

The taste of fingers is always startling, iron-y and foreign, like something that shouldn't be there. I was still holding the vibrator on me and trying not to get too lost in the feeling, trying not to slip away knowing having him would be better.

The more pleasurable my body felt the more numb my brain became. I was compliance personified. I was open to suggestion and ready to act, I wasn't in control and anyone who sounded more rational than me could take over. He built this trust in me slowly over time. He built it by always being hot for me, no matter how unflattering the sex position or sex act was. He built it by never failing to unconsciously soften his features when he looked at me. I always felt open to play with him. Sex didn't have to be a simple build and climax, we could do whatever we felt like, for as long as we felt like.

He removed his fingers, now coated in my saliva, and trailed them down my collarbone, between my breasts, and over my stomach.

"Please," I asked once more and his hands took over for my hands.

The way he looked at me as I begged him, it's what I always loved about him. He was so into me. Any response I had to him was the right response, he ate it all up and came back for more.

We could do this all night.

13

Mr. Fitzpatrick

"Blood, sex, and death." Those were the three things Mr. Fitzpatrick taught us were part of every gothic horror novel. He was the high school English teacher I hopelessly crushed on, and I couldn't help but notice that his eyes lingered on me when he said the second word. Sex.

I was a senior then, about to graduate. Glued to my seat even in the late, late spring when my classmates were terminally zoned out, focused on graduation, the summer ahead of them, college. But I still had unfinished business here, and today he was wearing a black tie over a light blue button-up and jeans that were just snug enough to drive my imagination wild. When he perched on the edge of his desk reading from *The Strange Case of Dr Jekyll and Mr Hyde*, I let my eyes wander up and down his body, imagining a new use for each part.

He was the new cute teacher this year, the one the girls whispered about between classes. Mr. Fitzpatrick is looking good today. I'd tried to pretend I wasn't one of them before, it's not interesting to have the same crush as everyone else. But his charm was undeniable, who else could make the classics so sexy? Every day when he taught, his inflection would bounce up and down with passion as he taught us about Bram Stoker and Shirley Jackson.

When he taught *Dracula* he became brooding and obsessive, delving into each character. Even in the clinical, fluorescent-lit classroom it was sexual. I spent the 50 minute class period imagining his lips — his teeth — on my neck, finding me in secret, lusting after my "life force" as Stoker says. The week he spent on *The Haunting of Hill House* was one of the most oddly erotic of my life. The text was thrilling, I was in a constant state of suspense and I held myself to not reading ahead, and being completely present in class when he talked about the role adrenaline plays in our bodies physiological state as we read. I didn't ask, but I was sure my increased interest in him was one of those byproducts he was talking about.

When graduation was only a few weeks away, I felt bolder. Surely I should make a move, if the consequences of being rebuffed were so low? What could they do? I was almost gone. And so I became consumed with the idea of hooking up with Mr. Fitzpatrick.

At first, I thought I could be subtle. Mr. Fitzpatrick certainly noticed when I wore something low-cut or a little more form-fitting. Once I entered his classroom in a dress that particularly accentuated my curves and I could have sworn I heard him groan. But understandably, he never did anything more than cast a lingering glance my way.

He'd get in too much trouble, I reasoned. I'm going to have to be the one to do something. So I put my mind into creating the perfect plan: I'd just have to present him with an opportunity he couldn't say no to.

The senior end-of-year dance was coming up, and I inserted myself into the planning committee long enough to serve as an official liaison and ask Mr. Fitzpatrick if he would be a chaperone, apparently we were in desperate need of one (I didn't ask anyone else). A light flickered in his eyes as I carefully enunciated the word desperate. Hopefully that was a look of comprehending my agenda. He agreed to the task.

I bought new lingerie, black and red and lacy. I wore it under a loose-fitting white sundress, pure and virginal like a gothic heroine, but dark and carnal underneath.

At the dance, I added a note to the clipboard waiting for him as a chaperone. It was the regular list of rules to enforce and emergency contacts. My note was underneath, it was a line from Dracula along with his room number:

> "No man knows till he experiences it, what it is like to feel his own life-blood drawn away into the woman he loves." CLC 345.

I never went to the dance. Instead I made my way through the dark and empty corridors of the school until I let myself into his classroom. I brought with me one candle to break up the darkness without relying on the fluorescents. Lighting it and setting it on a desk in the front row I climbed into Mr. Fitzpatrick's seat behind his desk, pulled the straps of my dress down so the top of my lacy bra was revealed, and crossed my legs with my heels resting on the edge of his desk, waiting.

It was a long wait. He didn't find my note right away, but it became pleasurably agonizing, every tiny sound I heard in the hallway seemed like it could be him approaching. I got excited and then mellowed again when I realized it was my imagination. When he did come, I didn't even hear him approach.

"Adrienne."

It was a guess he made as he entered the classroom, it was too dim to see my face but I had made sure the glow illuminated my nearly bare legs. I was glad he was expecting it to be me.

"Mr. Fitzpatrick." I acknowledged him and removed my legs from his desk, slowly crossing them in front of me.

"This note... what are you doing here? We shouldn't be here."

He was saying the words, but even to someone who wasn't engaging in wishful thinking they sounded unconvincing. He didn't want them to be true. I stood up and leaned against the edge of his desk, facing him, opening my legs a bit so he could imagine himself between them.

"Mr. Fitzpatrick, I'm sorry if you're misunderstanding. I just wanted to discuss *Dracula* more."

He moved closer, grinning.

When he was close enough that I could touch him, I grabbed his tie and pulled his body into mine. I could feel he was already hard as he pressed against the loose fabric separating us. The situation excited him as much as it excited me. "You've always been my favorite student, Adrienne, but I could get in a lot of trouble for being here right now."

Pulling harder on his tie, my mouth found his neck. "I'll just have to make it worth your while then."

He groaned and his hands found the undersides of my thighs, pulling me closer to him and moving us both back so I was resting on his desk. I slid back farther and wrapped my legs around him.

"I just wanted to experience this before graduation," I told him, "I've been trying not to make a move all year."

Even in the low light, I could see the smile that spread across his face. He says he loves the way I look lying on his desk. I respond by feeling the bulge in his pants, attempting to grip him through the fabric and feeling him grow.

"We need to make this quick. They'll look for me if I don't come back."

"Perfect." With the suspense building as long as it had, I wouldn't last long in his arms anyway.

I heard him unbuckle his belt and unzip his pants but I didn't look away from his face. Even in the dark he looked handsome, brooding. I wanted him to tell me more about sex and blood and death but I also just wanted to experience it with him — all the parts of being human, all the things worth writing about.

I was happy there, to be a willing participant in a fantasy I was sure he had. Happy when he slid the lace panties I'd brought for the occasion off, happy when he didn't bother to remove my bra but instead pulled my breasts free from it, and especially happy when his body met mine.

While forging a path with his mouth from my neck, down to my collarbone, and then landing on my breasts, he pulled me closer to him and entered me. The speed with which he poured himself into me belied his eagerness. I knew he wanted me as much as I wanted him to. As much as I'd fantasized about him wanting me.

Lowering himself so his face was next to mine he whispered, "Adrienne, if you want to be a great student you're going to have to finish me off with your mouth."

Kneeling before him, I skipped the niceties and began blowing him full on right away, working my hand around his shaft in tandem with my mouth. His hands worked their way through my hair, separating it into two ponytails he held firmly as he used them to guide my head onto his cock, increasing in rhythm until I felt him tense up, his hands clenching my hair. Pulling my head down on him, he held me there and emptied himself into the back of my mouth. I could taste the saltiness as I removed myself from him, licking my lips.

It was the perfect end to my senior year.

14

Sex Tutor

Brad wasn't my type at all. He just wasn't. He was hot, by anyone's standards. In his own vernacular, his body was "jacked." He was tall and broad-shouldered and his teeth were perfect and white and straight. He had the kind of blonde hair you'd expect to see in a movie about surfers in California. All this to say he was nearly perfect looking. But who can fall in love with someone who looks like a magazine?

I like brunettes, I like dark eyes. I like people who are complicated and brooding and the more

I got to know Brad the more I wondered if he'd ever had a bad day in his whole life. He was always smiling the same dopey, toothsome smile. We were lab partners in a chemistry lab neither of us had any business being in — except that we needed a science credit to graduate and this class seemed as good as any. The difference being that for me chemistry wasn't my thing but I could figure it out well enough to get by. Brad was lost. So lost he didn't know he was lost. Just oblivious to how he reached new breathtaking lows of intelligence day after day.

He was a bimbo, the worst of crimes in my book.

I have to admit I wasn't the nicest to Brad. I knew I was going to struggle in a science lab and while I fully intended to pull my own weight (as much as possible at least) I was hoping to get paired up with a brainy guy who could explain to me the things I didn't understand. I was fully unequipped to carry not only myself but this man who was unavoidably simple as well. And so I was curt. And condescending. And a little bit bitchy.

To Brad's credit, he always took my attitude with a smile and a genuine laugh.

Over the course of the semester he grew on me.

It was fun to have someone to take my aggressions out on with no consequence. Brad was so blessed in all the other areas of his life, I don't even think he realized I was being mean to him. Or at least he was mistaking my rudeness for friendship because we grew closer, barely scraping by on our weekly assignments. It'd be enough to pass, and it wasn't going to affect my precious 4.0 within my English major anyway.

When the final was approaching, Brad suggested we study for it together and it didn't even occur to me to disagree. He'd won me over with his indiscriminate happiness.

I arrived at his apartment to find him shirtless. Of course.

Staring at his abs, I lost myself a bit and made the cardinal college mistake of accepting a drink offer when I'm supposed to be studying. Of course I couldn't concentrate after that. Of course I lost interest in science completely — that's why that rule exists.

A few drinks in I got curious. Or rather, I got buzzed and gave voice to the curiosity I've always had, "Brad, can I ask you a question?"

"Yup," he responded, always eager, especially

when it seemed our actual studying was moving further and further away.

"Why do you let me be so mean to you?"

Brad looked serious for once. Like he was actually thinking instead of spouting off whatever came to the top of his head, "I think it's sexy."

Was I hearing him correctly? This bronzed adonis of a man thought I was sexy?

To be clear — I don't have low self-esteem but I happen to be aware of — and okay with — the fact I didn't look like the kind of girl Brad should be with. She was some Kendall Jenner of a thing — perfect looking (at least by this decade's standards) and free-spirited enough not to weigh him down with any thoughts that were too harsh.

I laughed. How could I stop myself? "YOU think I'm sexy? You're like the platonic form of sexy. Like, you have girls throwing themselves at you all the time."

I stopped laughing when I saw his expression, again he was serious. "I don't like them. They're all so... flimsy. I like strong women. I like how you boss me around when we do our lab together. To be honest, it's a big turn-on."

With this, I became very aware of Brad's hand on

my thigh, and how close we were sitting, and how my body was responding to his. Between my legs I felt the tug my brain wouldn't allow itself to give — approval of this simple but gorgeous man.

I'd never thought about this situation occurring — why would he be interested in me when his looks could get him a much hotter girl? Beyond that, I'd written him off long ago as "traditionally handsome but not my type" — how could a smart girl like me honestly be interested in such a bimbo?

But my body liked him, I could tell from the way his hand moving on my thigh was also moving a warm feeling up to my crotch. Fuck it, it's college.

I traced my hand down the outside of his arm, pulling it closer to me. He grinned that winning Brad smile and followed my invitation, climbing on top of me on the couch and kissing my neck lightly, causing brand new butterflies to form below my abdomen.

As hot as the beginning of almost any hook-up is my mind began to wander. Why is he kissing my neck so lightly? It tickles more than it feels hot. Maybe hot guys don't know how to do anything good in bed because they are used to girls throwing themselves at them? And then I realized, Brad liked it when I was bossy. Maybe I could just tell him everything I wanted to do and he would like it (and I would have an amazing time)?

"Kiss me harder," I instructed.

Immediately I felt the improvement. With a low, animal kind of groan Brad's kisses became more fervent, more impactful. I could feel his cock harden as it rested on my leg.

"That's good."

I ran my hand down his free arm and moved his hand until he was cupping me through my jeans. Apparently not as stupid at sex as he was at life, he caught on immediately and unbuttoned and unzipped me. I shimmied out of my jeans and his fingers went to work warming me up, his thumb rubbing my clit as he brought his middle finger inside me, sliding it down the front wall. I made sure to respond with enthusiasm to the area of my body he was clearly most gifted at touching.

"Now use your mouth."

I opened my eyes and looked down, trying to memorize the beautiful site of Brad positioning himself between my legs.

The fogginess of the alcohol gave way to the fogginess of oral sex, which is always so intense it's hard for me to keep a running thought process. I instructed him to use his fingers as he worked his tongue on my clit. I laid back and enjoyed his work, massaging one breast occasionally, trying to intensify the orgasm I knew was coming.

In those moments, I felt so powerful, controlling this hot guy, knowing that his entire aim was to please me, that he'd do whatever I said in order to accomplish that goal.

"Make me cum," I commanded him. "Go a bit faster and then don't stop."

Together his fingers and his tongue quickened and I felt an orgasm nearing. I massaged my breast again, initiated a full body tidal wave of an orgasm, bucking my hips a bit against Brad's mouth as it overtook me. Convulsing around Brad's fingers still inside me. Brad sat up, pleased with himself. No one could mistake such a full-body reaction.

I patted his hair as I put my jeans back on. "That was great, Brad. Can you get my books together for me now? I need to go to the library and actually study."

As I walked out of his apartment and towards the library my buzz from the drinks was completely gone, replaced with a new, better buzz — the high of having some kind of power over such a beautiful creature. We would definitely have to have more study sessions together.

15

MMF

When you have anxiety you tend to fixate on unrealistic doomsday scenarios. It doesn't matter how unhelpful worrying is, you find yourself unable to do anything else with the weight on your shoulders but try to think your way out of it. For years the source of my anxiety had always been the same: money. But now that I (finally) had a good job I naively thought I would get a break from the obsessive thoughts, that I would be able to relax, let my mind be blank for awhile.

Instead my anxiety just morphed into something

else. It shape-shifted into a new twisted little worry for me to spend too much of my time on: my health. I worried I was getting cancer from the two years in college in which I'd been an occasional smoker or that those lazy days at the beach would be the death of me, that skin cancer was a necessary consequence (and soon), and then wouldn't I feel dumb about how much I'd enjoyed myself?

"I'm young," I kept reminding myself, not even 30. Anything I had done to my body could be undone and whatever couldn't be undone at least wouldn't be helped along by my guilt about it.

As difficult as all of this was, it also put things into perspective. Puffed up, irrational anxiety worry or not, I was going to die one day so I better make sure I lived before then. The when may be an irrational worry but the conclusion itself was not. If the very worst happened and I went to the doctor and had a terminal illness, what would I regret? What would I immediately want to experience before things got worse? What was I holding myself back from because I assumed I would continue existing on into infinity?

There are wholesome things that come to mind, sure, but I'd never wandered far from those things.

I loved my family and spent time with them. I was always a generous and affectionate friend and girlfriend. I'd been lucky enough to pursue my dreams creatively. There was no big, stable thing I felt I had missed out on so I couldn't fault myself for a lack of doing everything in my power there.

I'm listing these things here to explain why the thing that really caught in my throat about dying was a pretty shallow consideration but it was present nevertheless. When I pictured that scenario my regret would be that I would wish I had had more sex.

Unlike the other areas of my life my desires and my actions here weren't aligned. I tried to avoid being "slutty." I turned down sex partners I could have enjoyed because I didn't want my "number" to get too high. I hadn't tried everything I wanted to try. This I would regret. I regretted it already.

I'd always thought I was a tough girl, single-minded even when it came to getting what I want. But suddenly I realized how arbitrarily I'd set aside what I wanted for silly fears about an imaginary reputation. I'd never let myself really consider living out some of my crazy fantasies — and for no reason more substantial than, "I'm afraid of what people might think if they found out." It was truly silly to think about.

So I decided to do it. All of them. The fantasies. I wouldn't wait for the bad news that would (probably) never come. I didn't need that to force me to live. I was going to experience the things I wanted and I would do it soon. Luckily, if you're a woman, sex — any kind of sex — is always available to you, no matter who you are or what you look like, so I didn't have to worry about that.

The first thing I did was to sit at my desk and make a list. (We modern women are all compulsive list-makers, no matter the nature of the to-dos to be cataloged.) I made myself write down everything I was interested in trying.

Sex Bucket List

Sex with a woman (well-endowed, long hair)
Sex on a balcony (people can see)
Sex with two men (not gay)
Sex with a much older man
Sex with a much younger (legal) man

Now that I made the list, it didn't even seem that bad or like that much sex. Some of these are downright prosaic, just uncharted by chance. They could be done, easily. Where to start? Which one was I most excited about?

I knew this, from the beginning. The real exercise here was one thing in particular, one thing I was careful not to admit always caused a particular kind of pleasant twisty sensation down below: I wanted to have a threesome. I wanted to feel my body pleasing two men. I wanted us all to lose ourselves in each other and be free for a night — doing whatever lust inspired us to do. The crux of it, being desired by not only one but two men who couldn't even wait for a turn of their own, was unimaginably hot. This is where I would start.

But who?

Until now I'd been passively hoping the situation would present itself. And it did, a few times. Once when I was sleeping with a guy in his hotel room and I knew his friend was "asleep" listening to us on the floor. But I was afraid to ask for what I wanted. (And, young women reading this, this is the surest road to having a load of deathbed regrets: being afraid to ask for what you want.) Another time a guy asked me, as we were fooling around, if he could go get his roommate. I remember viscerally how torn I was because I wanted to say yes but he'd had an after party which is why we were at his house and I knew in the morning while I figured out how to get home they might tell the bevy of men who'd crashed on their couches and it seemed like it could be unbearably uncomfortable. I didn't trust him, he was really into porn as I'd learned later and he was the kind of guy who boxed above his weight because of it, doing things he'd seen without knowing (or caring) how to really do them. As much as I wanted my threesome, he wasn't the guy.

I had two options. I could ask a guy I already knew and hope that was the kind of thing he was into, or I could find some kind of website or hookup app where I could ask people. Tinder was out because it's linked to Facebook and I want a bit more privacy than that for something like this. I finally settled on the idea of placing an ad on a hookup-specific website. I wanted to curate an atmosphere of complete lust that I wouldn't be able to achieve if I asked a random male friend. There was too much commonplace-ness in that relationship. It seemed dirty or even desperate, as I wrote the ad. Wouldn't it be classier to just keep meeting men in real life and hope the stars aligned for the blessed event to happen naturally? But I was done waiting, done leaving things to chance.

I got a lot of responses, as a any woman would, "a lot" by volume and not by quality. Only a few spoke in whole sentences and without cringey trashy colloquialisms and fourth-grade era grammar mistakes. The one I liked best read like an email from a friend. He sounded like someone I would know in real life. He said that he hadn't done anything like this before which was suspect, but hadn't I made the same claim and been truthful?

He said that he loved women and he loved sex and he wasn't embarrassed about it like a lot of men were (a thing which had always annoyed me). We're humans and we're self aware, but we're still animals and isn't it fun to give into our primal instincts once in awhile?

This is the kind of guy I could let myself go with. Not the judgemental polo-shirted men I knew in my waking life. The photo he attached didn't hurt either. Dark hair, dark eyes, tall enough to wear heels with, broad shouldered enough to feel small next to. We'd meet alone he said, naming a lounge in the next neighborhood over that was fancy enough to be an attractive date opportunity and dive-y enough to be approachable. Dive-y enough that the floors were cement but not dive-y enough that they were sticky beneath my feet.

We hit it off right away. I think any social interaction can be lubricated by the knowledge that unless either of you is actually appalling in real life the evening is going to end with sex. And it did. True to his ad he was animalistic — grunting like an unbridled man and directing the action like he wasn't self-conscious about his actions. He held my hips firmly beneath him and bit my neck as he forced himself into me. The sex was raw, passionate, good. I arched my back and screamed and none of it was performance, he made me lose myself into this act.

We laughed afterwards. How rare to find such a compatible partner. Most people were too timid for this kind of thing. Now we could focus on the task at hand: we needed a third. This should be easy. We'd be starting a fire with the kindling already aflame. No need to start from scratch. He had a friend he told me would do. Someone suggestible, he adopted the personality of the people he was around. We could show him how we wanted him to act. If we were passionate and lust-filled, he'd let himself be this way, too.

It was strange, to invite a stranger to dinner at my house with just his friend and a woman he'd never met. I would have thought I was some sort of a third-wheel if I was in his position but Peter promised me he didn't have a clue what was going on, he had just been promised a delicious home-cooked meal and was the kind of guy who'd endure a potentially awkward night for it.

But it wasn't awkward. The three of us clicked immediately, laughing through one bottle of wine and then two, and then three.

He was funny and sincere and a little bit combustible. He exploded with laughter — a huge laugh that filled the room and made everyone laugh harder. He complimented my cooking and my dress and told Peter he was jealous, where did he find such a woman?

As I got more of a buzz I let my compliments flow freely to him as well. I told him he was sexy and masculine, something every guy loves to hear. I sat in his lap while I filled his glass and fed him a bite of baked apple from my spoon. I wanted to start being obvious.

After dinner we took our party to my roof. Inside my furniture was modest but I loved sitting on the roof and watching the city lights so much that I'd splurged on a large outdoor sofa that comfortably sat us all. It was easy to make a move then, when I got up to fill another glass of wine instead of returning to the side of the couch I had been on, I straddled Ryan instead. I watched his face for a minute and then kissed him. I'd been searching all night for the answer to this question — is he into me, is he going to be okay with this? And his kiss gave me an unequivocal answer: yes.

Peter watched me make out with Ryan for a few minutes before he joined in, lifting my shirt up and slipping his hand inside my bra. My roof was somewhat private. I was sure that someone, somewhere could see what was happening, but both the adjacent buildings weren't tall enough to see onto it, so I felt comfortable removing my shirt and bra, giving both men a bit of a show.

At this point, I could tell Ryan was very excited by what was happening. His kisses became eager and he slid down my body to kiss one of my breasts while Peter kissed the other. It was a rare moment where I could tell I was getting extremely wet without being naked or feeling myself. I couldn't remember ever being this turned on before, ever being this carried away.

"You're so fucking hot," Peter muttered into my skin.

Lifting me off his lap Ryan laid me down on the couch and removed my pants. He opened my legs and began kissing my clit while Peter kissed my mouth. I couldn't focus on either of them, I could only respond naturally, moving my hips the way my body told me to move them.

Peter stood and brought his cock to my mouth and I lifted my head to put my mouth around it, trying to give him some of the pleasure that Ryan was giving me. It was easy to get lost like this, I didn't have any of the anxiety-thoughts or self-doubt that usually flickered across my mind while performing sex acts. I was too occupied with the business of pleasuring and being pleasured.

Eventually I stood and straddled Ryan, grinding into his cock while Peter stood behind the couch and I took him in my mouth. It was difficult to focus on both at the same time but Ryan's solid hands on my hips controlled my speed and after I picked up Peter's hands and deposited them in my hair, he did the same up top. I felt like I was putting on a show, and if I had any more room to be more turned on, that thought would have done it.

I was too preoccupied to notice Ryan was nearing orgasm until he had moved his hands to my waist, grabbing tightly and pulling me down hard. I felt him cum and collapse, exhausted with what must have been a surprising evening for him. Peter led me behind the couch and bent me over it. We let Ryan watch as we both came harder than we ever have before.

Surprisingly, both guys spent the night. Waking up happy and taking a minute before I remembered who was in my bed and why I was smiling, I realized what a waste it would have been if I'd never had this experience. It hadn't been awkward or sleazy like I'd worried, it had been freeing and fun and hot.

More things like this, I decided. I would do more things like this.

About the Author

I write porn for smart women. Follow me on Twitter @XOAdrienneWest and Facebook.

Printed in Great Britain
by Amazon

85336971R00082